For Peter and Laura with love
—A.S.C.

For Donavan and Beth
—T.A.

Here is a barn in the country.

Inside a Barn in the Country

A Rebus Read-Along Story

by Alyssa Satin Capucilli
Illustrated by Tedd Arnold

SCHOLASTIC INC.
New York Toronto London Auckland Sydney

ISBN 0-590-47000-0

40 39 38 37 36 35 34   6 7 8/0

Printed in the U.S.A.   40

Here is the mouse that squeaked
in the hay
inside a barn in the country.

Here is the that squeaked
in the hay

and woke up the horse that
whinnied *neigh*
inside a barn in the country.

Here is the 🐭 that squeaked
in the hay
and woke up the 🐴 that
whinnied *neigh*

that woke up the cow that
started to *moo*
inside a barn in the country.

Here is the 🐭 that squeaked
in the hay
and woke up the 🐴 that
whinnied *neigh*
that woke up the 🐄 that
started to *moo*

that woke up the rooster
cock-a-doodle-doo
inside a barn in the country.

Here is the 🐭 that squeaked
in the hay
and woke up the 🐴 that
whinnied *neigh*
that woke up the 🐄 that
started to *moo*
that woke up the 🐓
cock-a-doodle-doo

that woke up the chicks that
started to *peep*
inside a barn in the country.

Here is the 🐭 that squeaked
in the hay
and woke up the 🐴 that
whinnied *neigh*
that woke up the 🐄 that
started to *moo*
that woke up the 🐓
cock-a-doodle-doo
that woke up the 🐥🐥 that
started to *peep*

that woke up a couple of sleepy
white sheep
inside a barn in the country.

Here is the 🐭 that squeaked
in the hay
and woke up the 🐴 that
whinnied *neigh*
that woke up the 🐄 that
started to *moo*
that woke up the 🐓
cock-a-doodle-doo
that woke up the 🐥 that
started to *peep*
that woke up a couple of sleepy
white 🐑

that woke up the dog that
started to *bark*
inside a barn in the country.

Here is the 🐭 that squeaked
in the hay
and woke up the 🐴 that
whinnied *neigh*
that woke up the 🐄 that
started to *moo*
that woke up the 🐓
cock-a-doodle-doo
that woke up the 🐥🐥 that
started to *peep*
that woke up a couple of sleepy
white 🐑🐑
that woke up the 🐕 that
started to *bark*

Here is the 🐭 that squeaked
in the hay
and woke up the 🐴 that
whinnied *neigh*
that woke up the 🐄 that
started to *moo*
that woke up the 🐓 that
cock-a-doodle-doo
that woke up the 🐤🐤 that
started to *peep*
that woke up a couple of sleepy
white 🐑 that
that woke up the 🐕 that
started to *bark*
that woke up the 🐖 that snored
in the dark

that woke up the hens that
started to *cluck*
inside a barn in the country.

Here is the 🐭 that squeaked
in the hay
and woke up the 🐴 that
whinnied *neigh*
that woke up the 🐄 that
started to *moo*
that woke up the 🐓
cock-a-doodle-doo
that woke up the 🐥🐥 that
started to *peep*
that woke up a couple of sleepy
white 🐑
that woke up the 🐕 that
started to *bark*
that woke up the 🐖 that snored
in the dark
that woke up the 🐔🐔 that
started to *cluck*

Here is the 🐭 that squeaked
in the hay
and woke up the 🐴 that
whinnied *neigh*
that woke up the 🐄 that
started to *moo*
that woke up the 🐓
cock-a-doodle-doo
that woke up the 🐥🐥 that
started to *peep*
that woke up a couple of sleepy
white 🐑
that woke up the 🐕 that
started to *bark*
that woke up the 🐖 that snored
in the dark
that woke up the 🐔🐔 that
started to *cluck*
that woke up a very loud
honking old 🦆

that woke up the farmer

who sat up and said,

inside a barn in the country.